D0795645

No part of this publication may be reproduced in whole or in part, or stored in a retrieval system, or transmitted in any form or by any means, electronic, mechanical, photocopying, recording, or otherwise, without written permission of the publisher. For information regarding permission, write to North-South Books Inc., 1123 Broadway, Suite 800, New York, NY 10010.

ISBN 0-590-87172-2

Copyright © 1996 by Michael Neugebauer Verlag AG, Gossau Zürich, Switzerland. First published in Switzerland under the title *Teddybär*. English translation copyright © 1996 by North-South Books Inc. All rights reserved. Published by Scholastic Inc., 555 Broadway, New York, NY 10012, by arrangement with North-South Books Inc. SCHOLASTIC and associated logos are trademarks and/or registered trademarks of Scholastic Inc.

12 11 10 9 8 7 6 5 4 3 2 1   8 9/9 0 1 2 3/0

Printed in the U.S.A.   14

First Scholastic printing, September 1998

Brigitte Weninger
Ragged Bear
Alan Marks

Translated by
Marianne Martens

SCHOLASTIC INC.
New York Toronto London Auckland Sydney

Once there was a
big honey-brown teddy bear.

He was old and worn, ragged
and torn, but his heart was
still full of love.

He spent most of his time sitting in the corner, next to the old ball and the wooden locomotive.

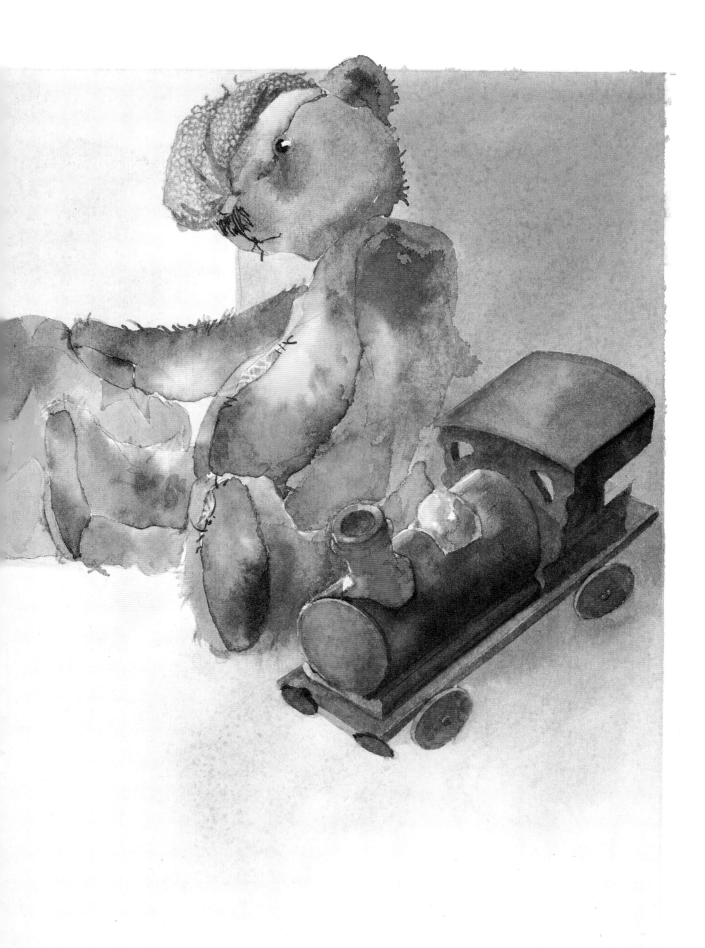

Once in a while the children would play with him.

They would throw him high in the air, until he landed with a loud thump!

That was fun!

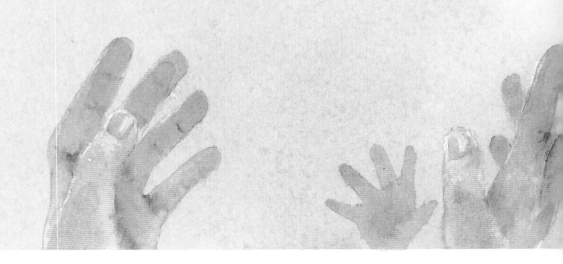

Sometimes they used him
as a pillow or as a doorstop.

Sometimes he was a tunnel
that the toy train drove under.

But when visitors came, the children would toss Teddy back in the corner.

They had much nicer toys to show their friends.

One day they brought Teddy
to the park. He rode in the tricycle
trailer with a puppet and a doll.

He was really happy.

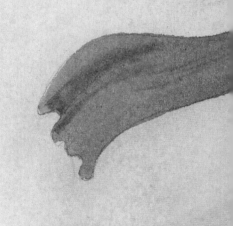

Then it started to rain,
and the children rushed
back home.

But they forgot Teddy!
He was left sitting on a park
bench all by himself.

Teddy cried, but because
he was already wet, no one
could see his tears.

He sat there for hours and
hours, soggy and miserable
and very, very sad, until
finally he fell asleep.

When he woke up, he was
being lifted by a smiling child.

Poor Teddy had looked so old
and ragged that someone had
thrown him away. But the
smiling child hugged him tight
and carried him to a new home.

There he was given a bubble bath, wrapped in a big towel, and set near the warm oven to dry.

Then he was lovingly brushed until his honey-brown coat shone like gold.

His nose was fixed, his ear
was repaired, and all the holes
in his stomach were sewn up.

And he was allowed to sleep in a bed!
He was hugged and cuddled, tucked
in tight, and kissed good night.

Later that night, as Teddy sat in the glow of the moonlight, he was the happiest teddy bear in the world. He was still old—and a little bit worn—but he was no longer ragged and torn. And his heart was filled with love.